CHOOSE YOUR OWN ADVENTURE®
titles in Large-Print Editions:

All-Time Best-Sellers!

CHOOSE YOUR OWN ADVENTURE® • 120

GHOST TRAIN

BY LOUISE MUNRO FOLEY

ILLUSTRATED BY FRANK BOLLE

An Edward Packard Book

Gareth Stevens Publishing
MILWAUKEE

For a free color catalog describing Gareth Stevens' list of high-quality books, call 1-800-542-2595 (USA) or 1-800-461-9120 (Canada). Gareth Stevens' Fax: (414) 225-0377.

Library of Congress Cataloging-in-Publication Data available upon request from publisher.
Fax: (414) 225-0377 for the attention of the Publishing Records Department.

ISBN 0-8368-1307-3

This edition first published in 1995 by
Gareth Stevens Publishing
1555 North RiverCenter Drive, Suite 201
Milwaukee, Wisconsin 53212 USA

CHOOSE YOUR OWN ADVENTURE® is a trademark of Bantam Doubleday Dell Books for Young Readers, a division of Bantam Doubleday Dell Publishing Group, Inc.

Original conception of Edward Packard.
Interior illustrations by Frank Bolle. Cover art by Bill Dodge.

1 2 3 4 5 6 7 8 9 99 98 97 96 95

Printed in the United States of America

For my friend, Lois Price,
who knows
we mortals do nothing
by ourselves

WARNING!!!

Do not read this book straight through from beginning to end. These pages contain many different adventures that you may have as you try to solve a mystery while spending the summer on a farm in British Columbia, Canada. From time to time as you read along, you will be asked to make a choice. Your choice may lead to success or disaster!

The adventures you have are the results of your choices. You are responsible because you choose. After you make a decision, follow the instructions to find out what happens to you next.

Think carefully before you act. Someone's been sabotaging the orchards late at night, and you've got to put a stop to it. Your investigations may lead you to a mystery of ghosts and Indian curses. But be careful. Even if you do discover who's behind the sabotage, you may not be able to save the farm.

Good luck!

You and your father were ready to leave on a trip to Canada's Okanagan Valley in British Columbia when the company he works for received a large contract, and he had to cancel the vacation.

The man you were going to visit, Harry West-lake, is your father's boyhood friend, and he has asked your parents to let you come anyway. Tourist season has started and Harry, the owner of several orchards and a fruit stand, needs some help. Harry's great-grandparents, you have learned, were among the first settlers in the area and planted many acres in peach trees. It sounds like a lot of work, but it also promises to be fun.

Your parents talked the situation over and have agreed that you can go and work for Harry for the whole summer! Now, five days later, you're on a plane flying north to Canada.

A tall, thin man wearing cowboy boots and jeans meets you at Kelowna Airport. "I'm Harry," he says, picking up your suitcase. "Glad you're here! I sure can use the help." He leads you to an old station wagon out in the parking lot. "Climb in."

He pulls out of the parking lot and eases into the traffic flow. "So, this is your first trip to the Okanagan?" he asks.

"My first trip to Canada!" you reply. "Okanagan is a strange name. What does it mean?"

Turn to page 2.

2

"It's kind of vague, like 'the Place of Water' or something. Okanagan is the name of the valley and of the lake." He grins at you. "Now ask me what Kalamalka means and I can tell you that!"

"Kalamalka?" you say, rolling the strange word over on your tongue.

"That means Lake of Many Colors. And now ask me who Ogopogo is."

"Ogopogo?" You're sure he's teasing you.

"Right, Ogopogo," Harry says. "And that's just his nickname. His real name is N'ha-a-itk. The Salish Indians named him."

"Okay," you say, grinning. You decide that if you're going to stay with Harry all summer, you'll have to get used to some teasing. "Who is N'ha-a-itk? And what does the name mean?"

"It means Sacred Creature of the Water, or, if you like, Lake Demon. He's the local pet." Harry turns down a side road. Ahead of you, the clear blue water of a large lake reflects the afternoon sun. "He lives in an underwater cave here in Lake Okanagan."

"You mean a sea monster?" you say. "You're putting me on."

"Nope," Harry replies seriously. "Many people have seen him. Last year some fellows from Hollywood even videotaped him. The most we know about Ogopogo is that he appears to be friendly."

You stare at the lake. Does Harry really believe in sea monsters? you wonder.

Go on to the next page.

"It's a big lake," you say.

"Eighty miles long," Harry says. "Plenty of room for a sea monster to hide." He starts the motor and pulls out onto the road. "I have a fruit stand just down here a ways, and the house and the orchards are up on that hill.

"House is too big for me," Harry continues. "It'll be good to have you there. Give the ghosts somebody new to pick on."

"Ghosts?" you say.

Harry grins. "Well, the place is old and creaky. Some of the natives say it's haunted." He turns the station wagon onto a narrow dirt road bordered on the left by a peach orchard.

"Wow!" you say to Harry. "Are these all your trees?"

"Not anymore," he says sadly. "Used to be that everything from the highway to the foothills was Westlake land. My great-grandfather bought it from the Indians. But this part belongs to the Naldo Corporation now. This'll be its last year in fruit."

"What do you mean?"

"Naldo is a development company," Harry says. "They're going to tear out the trees and build condos, unless I can come up with the money to buy back the land. My grandfather'd scalp me if he knew I'd sold those acres."

Turn to page 52.

4

"Don't worry, Chuck! It's just me!" you yell. You wave the lantern so he can see you. "I couldn't sleep. Came out to get some air!"

"Right," Chuck replies. "Just checking." He turns and goes off in the other direction as you breathe a sigh of relief. That was close.

You look at your watch. It's almost ten o'clock. The train is approaching through the north orchard, and the dog is on the track. Your timing is perfect.

You reach for the rawhide in your pocket and just as the dog leaps you toss it into the air. He catches the rawhide in his teeth. You grab the scruff of his neck and loop the rope over his head as the whistle blows for the third time.

You can see the brakeman's lantern swinging as the train slows almost to a stop. You pick up the dog and heave him at Saul as he leans out the door of the passenger coach. Jeremiah salutes you with his lantern as the caboose passes by.

The steam engine puffs along through the orchard below the house and then disappears. As you walk back up to the house, you're left with an empty feeling. You'd like to know what happens to the crew.

You climb the stairs to your room and put the lantern down on the hearth. You wonder if it still has the power to signal to the train in the other time zone, or if it only worked when the train was between time lines.

You take off your damp clothes and crawl under the warm comforter. You fall asleep instantly.

Turn to page 111.

6

There must be a loading dock at the end of this conveyor belt, you tell yourself. Even if it's not used anymore, the fruit that came in had to go out. If you follow the counter to the end, it should lead to an outside loading dock near the road. Maybe you can hitchhike a ride from there back to Harry's.

You climb up on the counter and crawl along the belt. You must be getting near the end. The grips on the belt have changed pattern. By the time it gets this far, you think, the fruit must be in crates, ready for the trucks.

Suddenly, you feel the counter moving slowly downward. You're on a weight-activated elevator! You feel a bump and swing off the counter. Free of your weight, the elevator slowly rises back up to the main floor of the packing house.

You shiver. It's cold down here. You feel around for the double doors that you know must be here. How else would they get the fruit to the trucks waiting at the loading dock?

Your hand brushes against a handle. You've found it! You push against the heavy door and step over the threshold. But you're *not* outside. You're *inside* a cold-storage locker! The door closes firmly behind you.

You are never seen again. Two years after your mysterious disappearance, the packing shed burns to the ground. Harry's fruit farm is subdivided, and condominiums are built on the property. Harry has a nervous breakdown, thinking he is the cause of your and Belinda's disappearances.

The End

Harry knocks loudly on the cabin door with his crutch. "Belinda!" he calls out. There is no answer.

You run to the window at the side of the building. "There are no lights," you say. "Maybe she's already gone. She said she wouldn't be here much longer."

"Did she say where she was going?" Harry asks.

"She said she was going to another place," you tell him. "She didn't say where."

"I'm not surprised," Harry says. He looks sad. "Take me to the sacred ground. I'll tell you a story on the way."

"But you can't go there!" you say. "Your leg . . ."

Turn to page 66.

You set the lantern down and chin yourself up to look through the window. Chuck and another man are standing by Harry's tractor. Chuck is holding a flashlight, and the other man is holding a small paper bag.

"Get the gas cap off," says the other man. "This will be our insurance!"

As you lean forward to hear what Chuck says, something hard pokes into your back. "Drop to the ground, real easy," a voice from behind you says. It's Harry, and he's holding a rifle!

"Harry, it's me!" you whisper. "There are two men in there!"

You hear a flurry of motion inside the barn, and a door bangs.

"Rats!" you say. "They must have heard us. They're getting away!"

Turn to page 22.

"Did Mariana and the farm boy get married after that?" you ask Harry.

"No," he replies. "When they found out that Mariana was here, the boy's family and friends came over screaming and yelling, demanding that my great-grandparents send her back to the tribe. But instead they hid her up here in this room while they tried to find her fiancé, with no success. They later learned that his uncle took him to Vancouver and signed him on as a deckhand on a freighter bound for Mexico."

Harry walks out onto the balcony. "This is the only reminder that's left," he says, squatting by the wrought iron railing. You notice that the metal is misshapen, as if it had been in a fire.

"What happened?" you ask.

"Oh, folks got nasty," Harry says. "Forget about it. You get yourself unpacked and come on downstairs. Supper will be ready soon."

Turn to page 21.

"Yes," she says, nodding. "Evil men. Bad for Mr. Harry."

"Are they the ones cutting the irrigation pipes?" you ask, helping her up. You feel guilty about having suspected her.

"Yes. I have put the curse of my people on them. They want me dead. You are also in danger. I see a shadow on your life."

"I don't believe in that stuff," you tell her. "Besides, those guys aren't very smart. They should have picked a better place to sabotage. Harry told me last night that the part from here to the foothills is the least productive land he's got. If he has to sell any more, this section will be the next to go."

A stricken expression crosses Belinda's face. "No!" she says. "He must not sell this. This land was sacred to our ancestors!"

Turn to page 30.

12

You decide that you must escape from Chuck immediately so you can get back to the farm and warn Harry. The road is lined on both sides now by dense forest. Up ahead you see a sharp bend. Chuck will have to slow down. You wait and watch.

The instant his foot moves to the brake pedal, you yank the door handle. Startled, he reaches over to grab you, but you're already out of the truck and tumbling down the gravel-covered grade at the shoulder. Tires squeal. By the time Chuck has pulled safely to a stop, you have disappeared into a gully, pulling leaves and brambles over you. From your hiding place, you hear Chuck crashing into the forest, grumbling to himself. Eventually, you hear the truck start up and leave.

You've succeeded! You crawl out, check the position of the sun, and start walking in what you think is the direction of the farm. But you are actually heading deeper and deeper into the forest.

In the fall, a deer hunter finds your remains. But the story only makes page five of the newspaper. The big news in the Okanagan Valley is the trial of Harry Westlake, who is accused of killing Chuck Simpson, the man he hired to guard his property. The newspaper reports that Harry shot Chuck when he discovered that the guard was being paid by the Naldo Corporation.

The End

14

Later that day, you walk up the hill to the motel where the doctor is staying. You want to thank him and ask him a few questions about the bite.

You go to the office. "What unit is the doctor in?" you ask the manager.

"Far as I know, there's no doctor here," she says.

"But I know there is," you tell her. "He's driving that big silver Olds out there. He saved my life this morning."

"You must have him mixed up with someone else," she says. "That car belongs to a salesman. Computer parts is his line. Look, there he is now, getting into the car."

"It's the same man," you say. "I know it is!" You open the door. "Doctor! Doctor!" you yell. But he gets into his car without even turning his head.

"He's not a doctor," the manager says. "I told you. He must just look like the doctor you want. It's just a coincidence."

"I don't think so," you reply slowly. "There's no such thing as coincidence."

You say good-bye to the manager. As you hurry back down the hill, you think of how you're going to apologize to Belinda for doubting her powers.

The End

It's Belinda! She's standing over by the pine tree in the yard, holding her rifle. Harry, alerted by the shot, comes out of the house on his crutches, clumsily carrying his rifle. The starter on the truck grinds as Chuck tries to start the motor.

"They're going to get away," you yell. "Stop them!"

"They go nowhere," Belinda says, nodding at the truck.

You follow her gaze. All four tires on the pickup are flat.

"I see Belinda's got things under control," Harry says, coming up beside you. He doesn't even seem surprised to see her.

"Harry! Where did she come from?" you whisper. "She's been gone for days!"

"Who knows?" Harry replies. "She comes and goes like the wind. But she always seems to be here when I need her, so I never ask questions."

Turn to page 105.

16

That night you let the crew of the ghost train know of your change of plans. The next few days pass in a flurry of preparations. You and Harry have targeted Saturday as the day for the Westlake Peach Party. On Saturday you're up before dawn, setting up booths and picnic tables and benches.

The first people arrive at nine o'clock, and from then on, cars line the road to the farm as hundreds of people come to the party. By the end of the day, they have consumed bushel after bushel of peaches and carried off hundreds of flats of the golden fruit.

When the last car has pulled away, you and Harry sit down at one of the picnic tables.

"I'd say that was a successful party!" Harry says, grinning at you. "By four o'clock I had enough to make the back payments on the mortgage . . . and I think I may even have enough to buy back the acreage from Naldo. That option was included in the sale, provided I could come up with the money within twelve months."

He looks over toward the front dock. "Did you hear something? A train whistle?"

You tighten your grip on the lantern, which you brought down this morning for the predawn setup.

"Probably just the wind," you say. Luckily Harry doesn't see you smiling in the dark, as you glimpse the faint yellow headlight of the phantom train coming through the orchard.

The End

"I'm afraid so," Frank says. "The dog you tried to save was hit by this train in 1905. The dog's owner, an Indian shaman, put a curse on us and the train. Now all we can do is keep shunting back and forth between your time zone and the time zone we came from." His voice drops and his eyes mist over.

"Until the dog is returned," Ben tells you, "we can't enter your time zone, and we can't go back to ours. We need your help."

"My help?" you say. "I don't see how I can help. I don't even know how I got here!"

"Your coal oil lantern got you here," he says. "That lantern fell off this train the night the dog was hit. It doesn't belong in your time zone. Folks in that big house must have found it out here." He picks it up and points to a name stamped into the blackened metal: VALLEY FLYER. "Just like mine, see?" He shows you his lantern. "As long as you have it, you'll be able to signal us and move between your time zone and ours."

"What happened to the dog?" you ask.

"I'm not sure, but after tonight, we know that he's alive and living in your time zone. If you can help us get him safely back to his own time line, the shaman will lift the curse and we'll be able to return to our families. Will you help us?"

Go on to the next page.

You look at their anxious faces and wonder how you would cope with being stuck between time zones.

"We won't lie to you," Ben says, "it could be dangerous. This shaman has great power."

"What's the shaman's name?" you ask.

"Belinda," Frank says.

Belinda! Can the strange old Indian woman really be the powerful shaman the trainmen are talking about? You're not sure you want to get too involved with her. On the other hand, you feel sorry for the men. You might be their only chance to return to their own time zone.

If you decide to help them, turn to page 106.

If you refuse to help them, turn to page 44.

That night you take your pillow and blanket out to the balcony and lie down. For a long time you count cars on the highway in the distance. Then you fall asleep. You've no idea how long you've slept when you sense that someone is near. You sit up and see a young woman wearing a headband and a cloth tunic standing beside you. Her long black hair reaches to her waist.

"Hurry! You must come with me!" she says urgently.

Are you dreaming, or is this really Mariana? What should you do? If you go with her will you be safe? Perhaps you'd better stay. If only you'd asked Harry what he meant when he said "folks got nasty."

If you go with the Indian woman, turn to page 107.

If you refuse, turn to page 38.

22

You run to the nearest door, fling it open, and stop dead. Chuck is standing just inside. "Who's getting away?" he says, grinning at you. "I'm just checking the equipment. We want it in top condition when we start picking tomorrow."

"That we do, Chuck," Harry says, hobbling over on his crutches, his rifle tucked under one arm. "Thanks. You can call it a night now."

Chuck looks perplexed. "Well, I'm not through with my rounds," he says. "I still need to check the shed by the fence and . . ."

"No need," Harry says, cutting him off. "We'll finish up."

You can tell that Chuck's not happy about being dismissed. He won't be able to finish whatever he was up to now. You pretend to be very interested in tying your shoelace for a few seconds in order to hide the big grin on your face. Harry must suspect Chuck, too!

Turn to page 104.

"Harry!" you yell, racing downstairs. "There's a strange woman burying something out in the back by the shed! She's got a knife! She may be one of the Naldo people."

Harry grins. "Dressed in Indian garb?" he asks. You nod.

"That's Belinda," he says. "She lives out there."

"Lives there?" you say. "But what's she burying?"

"Who knows?" he says. "She buries things out there and chants over them, but I don't pay much attention. Come, meet Mrs. Winters."

Mrs. Winters, Harry's cook and housekeeper, lives in town and commutes to Harry's every weekday. "Weekends you're on your own," she announces, as she takes off the big white apron that covers her short, plump body. "Harry's a rotten cook," she says, grinning. "I suggest you order in pizza on weekends."

You and Harry eat supper in a breakfast room off the kitchen.

"Tell me about Belinda," you say to him.

"Oh, she's kind of a strange one," Harry says. "I feel sorry for her. Some of the town ladies decided once that she was a threat to the community and needed custodial care, which meant locking her up in the township medical facility. So they got up a petition."

"What happened?" you ask.

Turn to page 42.

"That looks like Belinda's pouch!" you say to Harry.

Harry nods. "Do you know what's in it?" he asks.

"If it's the same as hers, I do," you say. "There's a feather, a peach pit, a clump of earth, and a rock."

One by one, as you name the items, Harry empties the pouch.

"What does all this mean?" you ask Harry.

"It means," he says, "that I don't have to sell any more of the farm."

"I don't get it," you say.

"You will," says Harry. "Right now, I must go and talk with Belinda. Come."

You pick up a flashlight on your way out. Your dinner plates, the food now cold, are on the counter where Mrs. Winters placed them.

"So it was Belinda," Harry says, almost to himself, as you walk slowly toward the picker's cabin. "I never guessed."

Turn to page 7.

26

"I'll help you check the pipes," you say to Harry. Meeting a saboteur sounds a lot more exciting than selling cherries, you think.

In the morning, Harry shows you how to repair damaged pipe by cutting out the broken section and gluing a new sleeve over both ends. The two of you leave to start your inspection.

"Watch for soggy ground," Harry says, as the jeep bounces along.

"That spot looks bad," you say, pointing to a swampy area. Harry pulls over and you jump out to inspect the pipe.

"It's been cut," you say. "I can fix this one. I'll run through the orchard when I'm done and meet you on the other side."

"Right-o!" Harry yells, driving off.

Turn to page 61.

You pick up the cashbox and go out. The pickup truck is loaded with boxes of cherries and apricots and early peaches for the stand.

"Hurry up," Chuck says. "At least that Indian woman got there on time. Didn't ride, always walked. Good four miles from the house, but she was prompt, I'll give her that."

"I'm usually prompt, too," you say. "I didn't know I was going to be working in the fruit stand until ten minutes ago."

"You were out late last night," Chuck says. "Snooping around with that lantern. If you're spying on me, you'll be sorry."

You start to speak but he cuts you off.

"That's what that Indian woman did. Followed me around. Never said anything. Just watched. Good riddance."

A truck passes you, and the driver flashes his headlights.

"That driver signaled to you," you say to Chuck.

"Never saw him before," Chuck says.

Turn to page 70.

"Halt!" Chuck repeats.

But you have more important things to do. The dog is crouched on the other side of the track, watching you. You reach for the rawhide in your pocket and toss it into the air. The dog leaps up and seizes it in its teeth. The train is coming closer. You grab the rope at your belt to loop it around the dog's neck. A shot rings out.

The next morning, investigators at the site try to piece together what happened. It's clear to them that Chuck mistook you for a trespasser and shot and killed you, but the real mystery is what happened to him.

One older detective scratches his head. "For the life of me, it looks like the poor fellow was caught by the cowcatcher on a train and dragged along the track here. Leastways that's what the markings on the grass alongside the tracks seem to indicate."

"But there's been no train on this track for fifty years, maybe more," says the other detective.

"I know," the older man replies.

Chuck's death is recorded as an unsolved mystery in the township records. The only witness to the events of that night is a yellow dog, who frequently returns to chew on a piece of rawhide that he has buried near the tracks.

The End

"I don't think that's going to have a lot to do with Harry's decision," you tell Belinda.

"It must! It must!" she says. She seems so agitated that you decide to change the subject. You look at the bundle she was carrying, which is now lying on the ground.

"What's in the bundle?" you ask her.

"Things I must take to the sacred ground of our people," she tells you.

"Where is the sacred ground?"

"On the moon side of the hills," she says, pointing beyond the orchard. "Only in the presence of the ancestors may the precious contents be revealed. Come with me."

You're curious to see the sacred ground she keeps talking about. But you can't quite shake your suspicions of Belinda. Could the tussle with the men have been staged? you wonder. Is this a trick to lure you to some remote spot? Or will you learn something that might help Harry?

If you go with Belinda, turn to page 85.

If you refuse, turn to page 89.

"I'd like a ride back to the farm." you tell Chuck. "Pick me up around five-thirty."

"I'll be here when I get here," he mutters.

You ignore his comment and start unloading the fruit. Your mind is focused on the Naldo truck. If Chuck is working for Naldo, that would explain why he hasn't caught anyone trespassing, and why you continue to find cut irrigation pipe. Hiring him as a guard is like hiring a fox to guard the chickens!

"Later," Chuck says, slamming down the last flat of cherries. He jumps into the truck and pulls out onto the road, heading back toward where the Naldo truck was parked.

You push aside thoughts of trying to follow him and tend to the business at hand. You lift the tray of bills out of the metal cashbox and put it in the wooden drawer. As you do, you uncover a drawing. You pull it out and examine it carefully.

On the left side of the paper is a sketch of an old truck with the Naldo emblem on the door. Beside the truck is a stick man wearing a baseball cap, much like the one Chuck wears. In front of the man is a pipe spurting water. In the lower right-hand corner is a drawing of a feather, like a signature. Suddenly, it's all becoming clear. Belinda was the only other one who had the cashbox. She must have suspected Chuck, too!

Turn to page 97.

You ignore the train and sprint after Belinda. You don't want to blow this chance to find out if she is the saboteur. She has a good head start, though, and she's moving quickly. Occasionally, you see her dark figure silhouetted by the moon as she hurries along between the trees. Is she trying to catch up with someone?

As the ground slopes down into a gully she disappears. Then the sounds of yelling and a motor fill the quiet night. You race to the top of the crest. One man is poised on a dirt bike, its motor running. Belinda is struggling with another.

You yell, running down the slope as the man throws Belinda to the ground and then jumps on behind the man on the bike. The driver guns the motor, and they take off.

"Are you all right?" you ask Belinda.

Turn to page 11.

"Gold," says Harry. "The spot where Belinda placed the rock marks the location of a rich deposit of ore. The shaman of the tribe back in my grand-mother's day knew it was there. He promised that the location would be revealed to whichever generation needed to know. I can't believe I almost sold that acreage!"

"Now you can mine the gold and pay off the mortgage," you say to Harry.

"Yes," he replies.

You look beyond the pass to the meadow, glistening silver in the moonlight.

Harry leans on one crutch and puts his arm around your shoulders. "I will protect its beauty," he says. "The sacred land of my people will not be ravaged."

"You read my mind!" you say, grinning up at him.

Harry nods. "Responsible people often think similar thoughts," he says. "Now, let's see if I can predict your next thought correctly. It will probably be, 'Let's go home and eat!' Am I right?"

You laugh. "Right! Let's go!"

The End

"The loading dock on the front road is too accessible to vandals," Harry tells you. "I don't know how long it will be until the strike is settled. I can't afford to put a guard out there to watch the bins. At least they're out of sight on the back road."

"But . . ."

"But what difference does it make?" Harry asks. "The fruit can rot just as easily on the back road as it can on the front."

You can't believe what you're hearing. It's bad enough having to figure out a way to load the fruit without Harry knowing, but how in the world are you going to do it if it's nowhere near the railroad tracks? You'd better come up with something fast. The pickers will be finished tomorrow.

You look over at Harry. He's got that stubborn set to his jaw that means his mind is made up. You wish you could tell him about the men and the train, but you gave your word. Should you try to convince him to put the bins at the front loading dock, without telling him why . . . or should you try to figure out a way to keep Harry out of action for a while? You remember Mrs. Winters' comment. Maybe Dr. Morrow could help you with that!

If you call Dr. Morrow, turn to page 114.

If you try to convince Harry, turn to page 84.

"Do you think Harry will sell his land?" you ask Mrs. Winters.

"He may have to," she says. "But he'll save the best till last. When I took coffee in, they were just dickering over that little back orchard up against the foothills"

Belinda's warning flashes through your mind.

"He can't sell that," you say. "I've got to stop him!"

You cross the hall and barge into the office.

"Aha! What have we here?" says a man standing beside Harry's desk. "Didn't anyone teach you how to knock?"

"You know better than to interrupt," Harry says, frowning.

"I'm sorry," you say. "But it's urgent. You mustn't sign anything yet. I need to talk to you first." You look at the two men, who are now glowering at you. "Privately," you add.

"Whatever you have to say," Harry replies, "say it now."

Mr. Fox and his attorney smile smugly at you.

"Speak up!" says the attorney. "What's the urgent news?"

You weigh the possibilities. Should you risk being laughed at and tell the truth—that Belinda, the 'crazy' Indian woman said not to sell that piece of land? Or should you make up a story that has more clout in order to stall for time?

If you tell the truth, turn to page 72.

If you make up a lie, turn to page 98.

38

"I can't go with you," you tell the young Indian woman. "I know I'm just dreaming. This is not really happening." Even as you speak, the Indian woman vanishes. You hear angry voices in the yard below.

You grab your blanket and pillow and return to your room from the balcony. Inside you realize that your bedding has changed somehow. The open-weave acrylic blanket is now a patchwork quilt, and the foam pillow is a flour sack stuffed with feathers. Fear crawls through your body. What is happening?

A rock crashes through the window as the mob below becomes more unruly. You run to the stairs and hurry down, but the door leading to the second-floor hallway is stuck. You push with all your might, but it won't open.

You run back upstairs. Something whizzes past your head and lodges in the mattress. An arrow! Attached to the shaft is a burning rag! Are Mariana's people in that mob down there, too? You slap at the flames with your hands, but the straw-filled mattress flares up like a torch, igniting the braided rug and the flimsy curtains at the window. In seconds the whole room is ablaze.

You rush out onto the balcony again. A howl goes up from the mob below. Flames eat away at the wooden flooring, searing your feet. The balcony is going to collapse! You're going to have to jump. Quickly you grasp the wrought iron railing with both hands and swing over the edge.

Turn to page 108.

"I'll work in the fruit stand," you say to Harry. "Will Belinda be there?"

"Yes," says Harry. "Will that be a problem?"

"No," you say. This could be your chance to find out what she's up to, you figure.

The next morning Harry drives you over to the fruit stand. He introduces you to Belinda and then leaves.

You turn to Belinda. "Harry says you're a member of the Shuswap tribe," you say.

Belinda nods. "Yes. My people live north of here. I do not see them much."

"Harry says you can put curses on people."

Belinda smiles. "The more one talks about what one can do," she says, "the less one is able to do."

"But can you?" you ask curiously. "Can you put a curse on me?"

Belinda turns away from you and looks off toward the mountains. "Spells are cast only with the blessing of the sacred spirits," she says. "We mortals do nothing by ourselves."

"I think it's all a bunch of hooey," you say. "Hocus pocus, mumbo jumbo."

Belinda turns to wait on a tourist. "Are you staying in town?" she asks the man.

"I'm at the big motel up on the hill," he replies.

As you pick up a wooden flat to move it, you wonder why Belinda is being so talkative for a change. Suddenly, you feel a sting on your hand. "Ouch!" you yell. "Something bit me!"

Turn to page 112.

40

You ride for a long time through heavy forests. Finally you see the outlines of houses in the village as you come into Sicamous. The train chugs to a stop.

"What's happening now?" you ask Ben.

"The men are unhooking the flat cars with the bins on this siding." He leans out and waves his lantern. "They're done," he says. "And now, we take off into our time zone, and you move back into yours. I'll need your lantern," he adds.

You nod, and you can feel tears filling your eyes. You know that this will be the last time you'll see the crew. "Good-bye," you say. "And thank you." You hand Ben your lantern and swing down to the station platform as the train slowly pulls away. As the cars pass you, the men wave—Saul, Jeremiah, Rusty. Suddenly, you do a double take. Hanging out of the caboose are two familiar figures: Chuck and his friend, firmly held in Rusty's grip!

"Figured we'd get 'em out of your hair for good," Rusty yells.

The train disappears, and you're aware of someone beside you.

"What's so funny?" a voice asks. It's Harry!

"Chuck and his buddy just took a trip that they'll never forget!" you say, laughing. "Come on, let's get these peaches loaded!"

The End

"Couldn't make it stick. They couldn't find a next-of-kin to commit her, and she wasn't threatening anyone. Only thing against her was that she was living on township land in an old lean-to."

"Is that against the law?"

"Yup. So I offered her the picker's cabin on my property. Couldn't stand to see her locked up on a technicality. I also gave her a job working in the fruit stand."

"Well, she certainly is weird," you say, still suspicious of the old woman's strange behavior.

Harry grins. "We're all weird in our own way," he says. "Belinda is Shuswap, a tribe from up north of here. She's one of the last shamans around. She inherited her grandfather's powers when he died."

"What kind of powers?" you ask. "And what's a shaman?"

"A shaman is sort of like a witch doctor," Harry tells you. "They can cure people, or put curses on them, or . . ."

"Put curses on people?" you say skeptically. "I don't believe it!"

"Once you've seen it, you'll believe it," Harry replies. "A few years back I saw a logger in Kamloops who had tried to strangle a young brave with his bare hands. The logger didn't kill him, but he messed up his throat enough that the brave couldn't talk anymore. Well, the brave's uncle was a shaman, and he put a curse on that logger."

"What kind of a curse?" you ask.

Turn to page 68.

You decide that you can catch up with Belinda later. Right now, you want to find out about the train and where it's going.

You run across the field. Puffs of steam come from the engine. The whistle screeches, then you hear another noise—a dog is barking angrily at the train. The animal has a large frame, but there's not much flesh on its bones. Where did it come from? you wonder. Harry doesn't have any dogs.

You whistle. "Here, doggie!" You whistle again. The train is getting closer and closer; the yellow dog is standing right on the tracks, defying the machine as it approaches. Your heart is thumping in your chest. The stupid mutt is going to get hit for sure! You leap for the dog, pushing it across the tracks just in time. The force of your tackle winds you, and you lie quietly for a few seconds, trying to piece together what has happened. You look around for the dog, but you don't see him. Everything is blurry. As your head clears, you feel a chill of fear. Faces crowd in around you, wearing concerned expressions.

"Where am I?" you ask.

"You're on the Valley Flyer," a man says. "I'm Ben Huggins, the engineer." He points to a man covered with coal dust. "This here's Frank, my fireman, and Rusty and Jeremiah here are my brakemen. And this is Saul, our conductor."

You start to protest, but the rhythmic sound of steel on the rails cannot be camouflaged. You know it's true. You're riding the train that hasn't traveled these tracks for over fifty years!

Turn to page 99.

"I'm sorry," you say to the trainmen, "but I can't help you. I've got my hands full already with Harry, his broken leg, and Naldo cutting irrigation pipe in the orchards. I just can't do it. It's too dangerous."

Ben nods sadly. "If that's your decision, we'll have to abide by it," he says.

The men go back to their stations. The engine shudders as the train backs off the siding. You grasp the lantern with one hand and swing down into the ankle-high grass of the field.

The minute you let go of the engine's handrail, the train disappears. But standing in its place is the angry dog.

With teeth bared, it lunges at you, tearing first at your arms and then at your head and neck. You try to fend off the attack, but you're no match for its violent frenzy. One well-placed bite opens your jugular vein.

Your body is discovered the next day in the field south of the house. But it's too late. You've already passed into another time zone.

And your coal oil lantern is still burning.

The End

"I'll take the attic room," you tell Harry. "If there are any ghosts up here, they'll just have to make room."

Harry grins. "Never met up with any myself," he says, "but folks coming down the highway at night used to say they could see lights up here. In fact, a couple of them thought the place was on fire and called the Fire Department. It was probably just Mariana, though."

"Who's Mariana?" You suspect that Harry is teasing you again.

"Mariana was a Salish Indian girl who lived in the valley about a hundred years ago. She fell in love with one of the farm boys, and they were going to get married. Problem was, the tribe didn't approve. And the family of the farm boy didn't like it much either."

"What did they do?"

"Well, the tribe got to her first; they set her adrift out on Lake Okanagan in a canoe."

"Did she die?" you ask, horrified.

Harry smiles. "No. My great-grandmother got wind of it. She went out on the lake, found Mariana, and brought her back here."

"That took courage," you say.

"Yes," says Harry. "Great-grandma was from the Shuswap tribe. Her own marriage to a white man—my great-grandfather—had worked. She thought the Salish should give the young couple a chance."

Turn to page 10.

"I'll walk back," you say to Chuck.

"Suit yourself," he says.

The day passes slowly. Only a few tourists stop to buy fruit, and you spend a lot of time thinking. You try to figure out why Chuck would accuse you of spying on him, and why the Naldo truck driver signaled to him. You keep coming to the same conclusion. Chuck must be working for Naldo. That night, you talk to Harry about your suspicions.

He pats your shoulder and says, "You know, sometimes when things aren't going right, we get to be scared of our own shadows. I know I hired Chuck on the spur of the moment, but I don't think we need to worry about him."

You're not convinced. One evening when you're out in the shed, you overhear Chuck on the cellular phone in his pickup. "Looks like about six days to me until old Harry has a FOR SALE sign on the lawn," he says, laughing.

You decide not to say anything to Harry, but to keep a closer watch on Chuck. Since the peaches are close to harvest, Harry tells you that he has hired a teenager to work at the stand so you can stay and work with him in the orchards.

"The Red Haven peaches are right on schedule," Harry says that night. "The pickers come next week. Looks like about six days will wind things up."

Turn to page 78.

You take a deep breath. "Harry, there's something I can't explain, and I'm not supposed to tell you about it, but I'm going to."

"Shoot," says Harry. "I can keep a secret."

"It's about the Valley Flyer," you say.

By the time you're finished telling the story, Harry is as excited as you are. "I have a hunch," he says, "that this crop is going to make it to market after all—strike or no strike!"

The End

You're riding up in the engine with Ben and Frank. You stare back through the darkness at the outline of the old truck.

"Something wrong?" Frank asks you.

"Well, yes," you reply. You turn to face the two men. "I told Harry about you and the train," you say. "It was the only way I could convince him to have the bins and the forklift on the front dock. I know he won't tell anyone, but I feel bad about breaking my promise to you."

"That's okay," Ben says, putting his arm around your shoulder. "In this case, you did the right thing. We asked you to keep it a secret because we didn't want to become a tourist attraction. Everyone would want to get their hands on that lantern."

"Well, there may be two other people who saw you."

"The pair by the dock tonight?" Frank asks.

"Yes, did you see them?"

Frank smiles. "We saw them, all right. Rusty caught one of them trying to pour something in one of the bins."

"I thought I'd frightened them off," you say. "Rats! That means they know about you and the time warp!"

"Oh my, yes," says Frank, with a smile. "They not only know about it, they're experiencing it first-hand! Rusty and Saul and Jeremiah are entertaining those two gentlemen back in the caboose."

"What?" you yell. You laugh so hard your sides hurt.

Turn to page 40.

The window is your only way out! If you can get to that other building, maybe you can hide there until they leave.

You pry at the catch on the bottom of the window. The rusty metal handle seems permanently stuck, but finally, squeaking and scraping, it turns far enough to free the latch. The window opens.

You look out to see if the coast is clear. There's no one in sight, and the evening darkness is closing in. You squeeze through the window and drop to the ground.

There are lights on in the main house, and a Naldo truck is parked in the driveway. You cautiously move toward the other building. A door slams, and you see shadowy figures moving beside the house. They're probably coming to get you! Staying close to the wall of the long building, you creep toward the door.

You're in luck! The knob turns easily; you push the door open and enter. It's cold and dark inside. You close the door and try to look around, but the building doesn't seem to have any windows and it's pitch black. You stumble. Reaching out, you try to grab something to break your fall. Your hand touches a counter with a conveyor belt on it. You realize that you're in a packing house!

Turn to page 6.

"If you don't like Naldo, why did you sell to them?" you ask, holding on as the station wagon bumps over some railroad tracks that seem to have appeared out of nowhere.

"I'd had two bad years in a row. I needed money to pay the mortgage on the rest of the land," Harry explains. "Naldo would like to get all my land. They keep sending their snoops around."

"Do you own a railroad, too?" you ask, looking back at the old tracks.

Harry laughs. "No, that's the old Valley Line. Used to run through here fifty years ago. Well, there's the house!" He points to a large stone and wood house up ahead.

Harry pulls the station wagon into a carport. The house is three stories tall, with balconies extending from some of the third-floor windows. You follow him into the front hall and up the stairway to the second floor. He pushes open a door, and you step into a cheerful bedroom, decorated in blue and white. A fireplace on one wall faces windows across another.

"It's nice," you say, setting down your suitcase.

"I'll show you the room upstairs, too," Harry says. "Hasn't been used much in the last fifty years. But you can take your pick."

He leads you through a door at the end of the hall and up a flight of narrow stairs. The ceiling of the attic room slants with the slope of the roof, and the windows open out onto a small balcony.

Go on to the next page.

"When I was growing up I'd often come up here and lie out on that balcony, counting the cars going by way over on the highway. My grandmother would never let me sleep in this room, though. She thought it was haunted. Don't believe in it much myself, but to each his own, I guess. Either room's as good as the other, but it's up to you."

You walk out onto the balcony as you try to make up your mind.

Off to your left an eagle soars effortlessly; beyond the orchards rise the majestic Rockies. The view is breathtaking. You don't believe in ghosts, and a room up in the attic would be really private.

Still, the other room was bigger. Maybe you should pick that one. Besides, it has a fireplace, and no rumors of ghosts.

If you choose the room on the second floor, turn to page 64.

If you decide to ignore the so-called ghosts and stay in the attic hideaway, turn to page 46.

54

As you watch from the window, Belinda starts walking quickly toward the orchards. Still watching, you slip your shirt and jeans on. She heads across the fields to the right. That's the area Harry was going to check this morning before the accident! Maybe your earlier suspicions were right. Maybe she is the culprit. Her knife is certainly sharp enough to cut through plastic irrigation pipe.

You grab the old train lantern from the hearth, then race downstairs and outside after the Indian woman. You don't want to lose her.

Suddenly you hear a shrieking whistle. You whirl around. You can't believe your eyes. An old-fashioned train is chugging through the orchard half a mile below the house. But it can't be! Harry said the tracks hadn't been used for fifty years or more. What's going on here?

You turn around just in time to see Belinda disappear into the trees at the edge of the orchard. She doesn't look back when the whistle blows again. It's as though she has heard nothing!

Belinda could be on her way to sabotage more of Harry's irrigation system. Harry will be home in a few days, and this could be your only chance to trail Belinda without interference. But you also want to find out more about the mysterious train. Where is it coming from? Where is it going? And why didn't Belinda seem to hear it?

*If you run to investigate the train,
turn to page 43.*

*If you continue to follow Belinda,
turn to page 32.*

Harry sits across from you in the breakfast nook while you tell him the whole story.

"And so," you conclude, "we need to put the bins at the front loading dock, because that intersects with the railroad track. And right now, the train is our only hope for getting the fruit to market." You look across the table at him. "Do you believe me?"

"Yes, because I want to believe you," Harry says. "And because you've never lied to me. You know, I swear I heard a train out in the orchard one night, but I thought I was dreaming. Sorry I forced you to betray a confidence, but I think that in this case, it was for the best."

"I guess so," you say, unconvinced.

Harry reaches over and touches your arm. "I'll keep your secret" he says. "Now we have some planning to do. Once the bins are loaded on the ghost train, they'll be taken to Sicamous. And that's tomorrow night, right?"

You nod. "Right. Then when we get to Sicamous, I can take the fruit through the time warp and we can load it into a refrigerated car going to Vancouver."

"I can help with that," Harry says. "I'll wait in Sicamous to take delivery. And I'll arrange for the refrigerated car."

"Thanks for not telling me I'm crazy," you say, grinning at him.

"That doesn't mean you're not," he answers, patting your shoulder. "Let's turn in. We have a big day ahead of us tomorrow."

Turn to page 75.

You grab the lantern in one hand and climb up the side of the bin, carefully lowering yourself into a corner on top of the fruit. You whistle softly.

"What's that?" Chuck says.

"I didn't hear anything," his friend replies.

Grinning, you whistle softly again, and fire off three peaches in the direction of their voices. When you're sure you have their attention, you light the lantern and raise it over your head. You wave it back and forth, hoping the train crew will also see its light.

"What's that light?" Chuck asks. "Up there, in the bin!"

"Somebody's up there," says the other man, moving toward the pickup. "We're going to be caught red-handed! Let's get out of here!"

You wave the lantern at the train again before you swing down from your perch. The train slows and then stops beside you.

"Right on schedule!" Ben says, jumping down. "Let's get those peaches loaded!"

The trainmen gather around the forklift, good-naturedly arguing about who gets the first turn at running this new and wonderful machine. It doesn't take long to get the bins loaded on the flat cars.

"All aboard," Saul yells.

The whistle blows, the train shudders, and slowly it starts moving its precious cargo north toward Sicamous. Not until you've cleared the dock do you see that the pickup is still there.

Turn to page 49.

"Sit down!" you yell. "You're going to tip the boat!" But your warning comes too late. The canoe flips over, and you are thrown into the cold, churning lake. You flail in the water for a moment, then tread water as you look around for Mariana.

"Mariana!" you call, squinting through the darkness. The water is cold, and you struggle to keep yourself afloat. To your right you make out the overturned canoe. Mariana is clinging to the hull. You swim toward her and grasp the side.

"Are you all right?" you ask.

"The great N'ha-a-itk has saved us," Mariana says.

"You mean, Ogopogo?" you mutter, remembering what Harry told you. "I'm not sure he had anything to do with it."

"You must not say that!" Mariana says. "Or the Great One will take back his benevolence!"

You start to argue the point but are interrupted by her shout. "Look! A rowboat!"

"Help!" you yell. "We're over here!"

As the rowboat comes closer, you can see that its occupant is an Indian woman. She pulls up alongside and helps the two of you into the boat. She and Mariana exchange a few words in Indian dialect, then she turns to you.

"The great N'ha-a-itk has looked on you with favor."

"I don't know about Ogopogo the water monster," you say with a grin, "but it sure was handy having that overturned canoe close enough to hang on to."

Turn to page 91.

"Sure I'll come along. I'd like to see the orchard," you tell Harry.

After dinner you help Harry load some plastic piping and tools into an old jeep. Soon you're bouncing over rutted trails leading through the orchards, headed toward the farthest lot.

"There's more railroad tracks," you say, holding on to the seat. "Are these tracks connected to the ones we crossed on the way in?"

"Yup. The Valley Line ran right through here. Track's all overgrown now. Like I said before, the line hasn't been used for fifty years, maybe longer. My dad used to tell me that when he was a boy he'd listen for the steam engine whistle and then run to wave at the engineer."

"Where did the line run?" you ask.

"Up to Sicamous. All the growers shipped their produce out on the Valley Line. More dependable than what we've got now, if you ask me."

"What do you mean?"

"The truckers," Harry says. "They're threatening to strike again. 'Course, if the trucking companies would pay them a decent wage, those fellows wouldn't have to strike. But no matter who's to blame, if there's a strike, I'll lose everything."

"Everything?" you ask. "You mean the peach crop?"

"I mean *everything*," Harry repeats. "Orchards, house, everything. If I lose the crop, I can't pay the mortgage. If I don't pay the mortgage, Naldo has an option on the whole place."

Turn to page 82.

It doesn't take you long to replace the pipe. Soon you're jogging through the orchard to meet Harry. Suddenly a sharp noise rips through the morning quiet. It sounds like a rifle shot! You stop and listen, circling up the side of a small hill so you can look down into the valley below. Now it's obvious that what you heard was a tire blowout. The jeep is tipped over and Harry is lying motionless beside it.

"Harry!" you yell, sprinting down the slope. "Harry!"

His eyes flutter open and then close. "My leg," he whispers.

His right leg is twisted at the knee at a grotesque angle. "It looks like it's broken, Harry," you say. "I'd better not try to move you. I'm going back to the house for help." You grab a blanket from the back of the jeep and spread it over him. "Try to lie still. I'll hurry!" you promise.

You run back to the house. Mrs. Winters calls for an ambulance and a tow truck. Harry is taken to Valley Hospital where his leg is set and put in a cast. The doctor says it will be several days before he can come home.

Turn to page 73.

62

"I don't get it," you say to Harry. "How would cutting a few pipes help someone get your land?"

"If those trees don't get water during the critical period, there'll be no crop. Controlled watering is the only way."

"Why don't we take turns watching for trespassers at night?"

Harry pats your shoulder. "It's a good idea," he says, "but I've got miles of irrigation pipe out there. It would take an army to watch it. We'll just have to spot-check."

"I can watch from my room at night with those binoculars."

Harry nods. "It couldn't hurt," he says. He locks the barn door and the two of you walk to the house. Belinda has disappeared, and the bonfire is now ashes.

"Do you think Belinda might have cut the pipe?" you ask.

Harry looks at you quickly. "No!" he says. "Why in the world would she want to do that?"

"Well, you said this was land that originally belonged to her tribe. I thought that maybe . . ."

Go on to the next page.

"The whole valley belonged to the Indians," Harry says. "Not just my land. Belinda's got no reason to sabotage me. I'll check for other cut pipes in the morning. You can come with me or work in the fruit stand."

You're not convinced that Belinda isn't behind the sabotage. If you work in the fruit stand, you'll have a chance to size her up, and maybe prove that she's the culprit. But the irrigation system is extensive, and Harry could probably use your help checking the pipes.

If you go with Harry, turn to page 26.

If you work at the fruit stand, turn to page 39.

"I'll take the room on the second floor," you tell Harry. "I've never had a fireplace in my bedroom before."

Harry chuckles as you go back downstairs. "Back when my great-grandfather built this house, fireplaces were the only heat they had." He opens the door to the blue and white room. "This was his favorite room. My grandfather's, too. I think they liked it because they could see so much of the estate from here. My grandfather spent hours at that window squinting into those binoculars."

A phone rings downstairs, and Harry goes out to the hall. "Get unpacked," he says. "I'll see what Mrs. Winters has planned for supper."

You close the door and look around. On the fireplace hearth is an old coal oil lantern, just like one you saw in a railroad museum once. Good to have in case a storm cuts off the power, you think. You go to the window. The afternoon sun outlines the mountains beyond the orchards to the west.

Someone comes out from behind a shed that stands between the house and the orchard. You pull aside the curtains and pick up the binoculars for a better look. It's a woman dressed in a long skirt, with a band of cloth around her forehead. And she's holding a wicked-looking knife!

The woman squats down and digs a hole in the clearing. She appears to be burying something. But what? Could she be one of the Naldo Corporation troublemakers that Harry told you about?

Turn to page 23.

66

"I must go to the sacred ground," Harry tells you. "I can make it if you'll help me." He slips the leather drawstring of the pouch around his wrist, and the two of you start off down the road to the orchard. "This pouch," he says, "was given to me by my grandmother. Her mother, my great-grandmother, was of the Shuswap tribe. She told me that when the sacred tribal land was in jeopardy, the ancestors would send a messenger. The messenger would have a pouch like this."

"So Belinda was the messenger!" you exclaim. "And you're part Shuswap! So when she said 'our' ancestors, she meant yours, too!"

Harry nods. "But I didn't know where the sacred land was."

You are almost to the pass that opens into the meadow now.

"Here it is," you say to Harry.

Harry stares at the meadow bathed in moonlight. Then he turns to you. "Where did she put the rock?" he asks.

You walk to the mouth of the pass and pick it up. "Here."

"Please hand it to me," Harry says.

He takes the piece of rock you hand him and the one from his leather pouch and pieces them together. The broken edges match perfectly. "Shine your light over here," he says.

You aim the beam down on the rocks in his hands.

"What's that shiny stuff?" you ask, staring at them.

Turn to page 34.

Metal wheels screech on metal rails as the engine slows to a halt. Ben waves from the cab, and you grab the ladder and pull yourself up as Saul and Jeremiah hurry through from the back.

"Good to see you again!" Ben says. Frank grabs your hand, and Rusty gives you a hug. "What's the occasion?"

As briefly as you can, you explain to the men about the trucker's strike and how Harry will lose not only the crop, but his orchards as well if he can't get his peaches to the coast.

"I don't get it," says Rusty. "We can get the peaches to Sicamous, but that's the end of the line. How do they get to the coast from there?"

"Well," you say slowly, "if you can get them to Sicamous and unloaded, I'm hoping I can arrange to get them loaded into a Canadian Pacific refrigerated car for the rest of the trip."

"What's a refrigerated car?" Rusty asks, puzzled.

He grins when you explain and shakes his head. "Boy, could we use something like that!" he says.

"Do you think it'll work?" you ask Ben.

"Only one way to find out!" he replies. "Where do we pick up the fruit?"

"The road out to the highway crosses the tracks at one spot," you say. "I'll have the bins stacked beside the road. The forklift driver will think they're for truck pickup if the strike ends. I just hope Harry doesn't ask any questions."

Turn to page 77.

"He put a curse on the logger's hands," Harry says. "The fellow's hands got all crippled up, with fingers bent in and knuckles stiff . . . in a position like he was about to strangle somebody. He can't move his fingers, can't work his job, can't pick anything up, can't even feed himself. So don't you go pooh-poohing a shaman's curse. They can be powerful."

Harry changes the subject and starts talking about the orchards and the fruit stand, but your mind keeps returning to the woman by the shed and the strange powers that Harry talked about. What in the world was Belinda burying?

As you finish your supper, Harry says, "Think I'll go out to the west orchard after supper to check the irrigation pipe. Do you want to come along?"

You think for a minute. You do want to see the orchard, but you'd also like to keep an eye on this Indian witch doctor and try to find out what she buried.

If you go with Harry, turn to page 59.

If you stay at the house, turn to page 80.

In the morning, you're glad that Harry isn't there to see the damage. As Belinda predicted, the crop did not survive. You take a bicycle from the equipment barn and ride from orchard to orchard. Branches are torn from trees, and immature fruit is strewn on the ground like small green pellets.

When Harry comes home from the hospital the next day, you and Mrs. Winters fix a bedroom for him downstairs in his office.

You spend most of the day in the orchards, picking up fallen branches and pruning off those that hang like wounded appendages from the trees.

When you get back to the house, Harry is talking to someone in the office. You take a shower, then wander out to the kitchen to see if dinner is ready. Mrs. Winters is about to leave.

"Everything's ready to dish up," she says. "But don't go in there until his company leaves." Her tone is disapproving.

"Who's in there?" you ask.

"Bert Fox and his city slicker attorney, that's who. A couple of vultures. They arrived before the last hailstone melted."

"Who's Bert Fox?" you ask.

"President of the Naldo Corporation," Mrs. Winters says. "He wants to buy every piece of land in the township."

Turn to page 37.

70

Your intuition tells you he's lying. Two miles down the road you know you're right when you see the same truck parked on the shoulder. The driver is standing beside the vehicle, waving as you approach. Chuck ignores the man and drives quickly past, but not before you've seen the red and black Naldo emblem on the truck. Why would a Naldo driver signal Chuck?

"You walking back or you expect me to come and get you?" Chuck asks.

Walking back sounds a lot more pleasant than riding with Chuck again. On the other hand, if you ask for a ride you might be able to learn why the Naldo driver was flagging him.

If you ask Chuck to pick you up,
turn to page 31.

If you say you'll walk back, turn to page 47.

"Speak up," Harry says to you. "What's so urgent? What do you need to tell me?"

You take a deep breath. You know what reaction the other men will have, but you must give Harry Belinda's message. "Belinda said to tell you not to sell that piece of land," you say.

Mr. Fox clears his throat, and the attorney covers his mouth with his hand to hide a grin. But Harry isn't laughing. "Tell me exactly what Belinda said," he says to you.

"She said the land was sacred to your ancestors."

"Her ancestors, you mean."

You stop to think. "No, she said 'our' ancestors, as though they were your ancestors, too. She took me to the sacred ground."

"Are you now taking your financial advice from a Shuswap squaw, Mr. Westlake?" the attorney says.

Harry turns to face the man. "I am," he says. He points to the office door with his crutch. "Good evening, gentlemen. Our business is over." He closes the door firmly behind them.

"Tell me everything," Harry says. "What did you see at the sacred ground? Where is it?"

You tell Harry about the mountain meadow and the bundle Belinda carried.

"A bundle?" Harry says, his face turning pale.

Moving awkwardly on his crutches, he goes to his desk and sits down. He reaches far back into a drawer and pulls out a leather pouch. It looks exactly like Belinda's.

Turn to page 24.

The jeep is towed to the equipment barn. "No point in trying to fix that tire," the tow truck driver says. "The shot went through both walls."

"Shot?" you say. "I thought it was a blowout."

"Nah, it was a rifle. I'd stake my paycheck on it."

"But who'd want to shoot at Harry?" you ask.

The driver shrugs. "Who knows. Could have been tourists after some game out of season, or kids taking target practice."

You don't tell Mrs. Winters that the tire was shot. She's nervous enough already. "I don't like the idea of you staying alone in this big old house," she says. "Only person around is that Indian woman, and she's kind of strange. Why don't you stay with Mr. Winters and me in town until Harry gets home?"

"I'll be fine," you tell her. "I don't mind staying alone."

But that night, when you're up in your room trying to read, you aren't quite so brave. The quietness of the house becomes like another presence. And then you start to hear things. Running water. Footsteps. Whispers. Is someone outside?

You grab the binoculars and creep over to the window. The moon is bright, and you focus on a shadow over by the shed. It's Belinda! She stoops to pick up a bundle and you see the flash of her knife, slipped into her belt at the hip.

Turn to page 54.

By sundown the next evening, all the bins are lined up at the front loading dock. Harry leaves right after dinner for Sicamous.

"I'll meet you up there," he says. "It'll be good to get behind the wheel. Awkward with this cast, but I'll make it."

The house is deadly quiet after he leaves. You try to read but can't concentrate. Finally you get the lantern and go out to the loading dock to wait. You've been there about an hour when you notice a vehicle turning off the highway onto the side road. Your heart begins to pound. Who could be coming at this hour? It's almost time for the train!

You look off across the field and, sure enough, far in the distance you see the flickering headlight of the Valley Flyer.

The approaching vehicle is a pickup truck, and its lights have been turned off. You extinguish the lantern and crouch behind a bin as the truck pulls up to the dock.

"Wouldn't water work just as well?" a voice asks.

It's Chuck's voice, and there is another man with him.

"Won't work as fast as the chemical," says the other man. He laughs. "If we pour just one gallon of this stuff in each bin, Harry will have tons of rotten peaches by morning."

Harry's fears were right! They're going to sabotage his fruit! You must stop them. It will be only minutes until the train gets here.

Turn to page 57.

Above the sound of the wind and the waves, you hear Mariana crying softly.

"Don't cry, Mariana," you say. "We have to think of a way out of this mess!"

"There is no way out," she says. "My love has gone. His people have sent him to the end of the world, where the water is deep and continues forever."

You guess from her description that she is talking about the coast and the Pacific Ocean. "I'm sorry," you say. Large waves are rocking the canoe, and the cold lake water is splashing in. "Mariana, we have to free ourselves before we capsize. Turn around so I can reach the bindings on your wrists."

Mariana pivots around until your fingers can reach the ropes. You struggle with the wet knots. The rough hemp scrapes the skin from your fingers, but you finally manage to release her hands. Then you turn around and she unties yours.

"You grew up by this lake," you say. "Where is there a cove? We must find shelter. The storm is getting worse."

"We have no paddle," she says.

"We'll paddle with our hands," you say, knowing as you say it that hand-paddling is not going to get you very far. Rain pelts down as the boat is tossed on the waves.

"Only N'ha-a-itk can save us," Mariana says. Abruptly, she stands up. "I call on you, Oh Sacred Creature of the Water!"

Turn to page 58.

"How do we load these bins?" Rusty asks.

"You'll need to bring flat cars," you say. "And I need to figure out a way to have the forklift there."

"We'll be glad to give it a try," Ben says.

"Thanks," you say, shaking his hand. "I knew I could count on your help. See you Thursday night!"

You swing down to the ground, gripping the lantern tightly in one hand. The train, which has been idling, picks up steam and starts forward.

You know that there is still a lot of work to be done, but you feel better than you have in days. You turn and start for the house, but you haven't gone three steps when you see a light flash over by the equipment barn. You blow out the lantern and carefully make your way across the clearing behind the house. When you reach the barn, you creep alongside the wall until you find an open window. Voices from inside tell you that there's more than one intruder.

Should you risk confronting them by yourself, or should you go back to the house and tell Harry?

If you confront the intruders, turn to page 9.

If you go to the house and tell Harry, turn to page 86.

Six days! You remember what Chuck said on the phone. You know that Harry's looking forward to getting the crop in, but what is Chuck anticipating with such pleasure? You can't figure it out.

On Sunday evening, Harry gets a phone call from one of the other fruit farmers in the area. You can tell by watching his face that the news isn't good. After he hangs up, he hobbles over to the window on his crutches and looks out at the rows of trees outlined by the setting sun. "I may lose it all yet," he says.

"What's happening?" you ask.

"The truckers voted to strike," he replies.

"So what do we do now?" you ask.

"The fruit's ready," Harry says. "We have to go ahead and harvest as planned. But it may just sit in the crates and rot."

"Isn't there another way to move it out?" you ask.

Harry shakes his head. "There isn't a trucker in the province who'll cross the picket line. The only way to get the fruit to the coast in good condition would be by train from Sicamous." His shoulders sag as he lowers himself into a chair. "But getting it to Sicamous without trucks would take a major miracle."

Turn to page 95.

"Out," Chuck says, when you reach the building. You follow him inside. There are six bunks in the main room, and it smells musty, as if no one has been in it for a long time.

"This way." Chuck leads you to a door marked INFIRMARY. "In you go," he says, giving you a shove. The door slams behind you and you hear the key turn in the lock.

There's a cot in the room, and a small desk and chair. A narrow window, about two feet deep, rims one wall at ceiling height. You climb onto the desk so you can look out. You can't see the house from where you are, but within view is another long, low building, bigger than the one you're in.

You get down and sit on the cot to think. Chuck said 'until dark' to the man in the truck. That must mean that he's planning to take you somewhere else tonight. You have to get out of here! You go to the door and throw all your weight against it, but it doesn't budge.

Turn to page 51.

80

"I think I'll stay here and finish unpacking," you say to Harry.

"Suit yourself." He gets up from the table and leaves.

You watch from the window until Harry drives down the orchard road. Then you hurry outside. You don't believe any of that shaman's curse nonsense that Harry was talking about, but you are curious about what Belinda was burying.

You approach the picker's cabin cautiously. It seems to be deserted. You go to the place where you saw Belinda digging and drop to your knees.

You dig with your hands for several minutes, but you don't uncover anything. You know she buried something—right at this spot. Just then a gleam of silver flashes in front of you—Belinda's knife! It's suddenly embedded in the ground, inches from your hands.

You turn. Belinda is standing behind you. Beside her, dancing on a patch of bare ground, is a strange, golden light.

"What is that?" you ask apprehensively. You know it's some sort of trick, but it's very spooky.

"The ancestral spirit, come to reclaim the land," she says.

"I don't believe in spirits," you say, following the bobbing light with your eyes. It moves closer. You shrink away.

Turn to page 92.

Harry brakes, and the jeep bounces to a stop.

"Give me a hand," he says, hoisting a length of pipe from the rack on the jeep. "That line over there is cracked."

You watch as he drops to his knees on the soggy ground, slices out the damaged pipe, and glues in a new joint and section. He slides the damaged piece toward you. "Put it on the rack."

You and Harry check two more spots and then head back to the house. A small bonfire is burning near the spot where Belinda was digging earlier, and she is on her knees beside it bowing back and forth and chanting.

"What's she doing?" you whisper to Harry.

"Don't know, don't care," he says. "If she wants to tell us, she will."

"What do you think she buried out there tonight?" you ask, unwilling to let the subject drop.

"That's her business, not ours," says Harry, steering the jeep into the barn. "Our business is this pipe." He takes the pipe off the rack and lays it on a workbench under a fluorescent light. "Just what I thought," he says, turning it over.

"What?" you ask.

"It's not cracked," says Harry. "This isn't weather stress. This pipe's been cut."

"Who'd want to do that?" you ask as Belinda's knife flashes into your mind.

"The people who want my land," Harry replies grimly.

Turn to page 62.

Chuck watches silently as you finish loading the fruit. Then the two of you get into the truck. He pulls out onto the highway and steps on the accelerator.

"Where are we going?" you ask. "This isn't the way back to the farm."

"No, it isn't," Chuck says to you. "You know too much now. I can't let you go back to Harry's. I'm taking you to see the real boss."

There's no doubt in your mind now that Chuck is on the Naldo payroll. And there's no doubt in your mind that you're in great danger.

Should you try to escape now? If you're going to warn Harry, there's no time to lose. Chuck is only one man, and who knows how many of his cohorts will be waiting at the other end?

Escaping from the truck may be difficult, though, especially at the speed Chuck is driving. Maybe it would be better to wait until you reach your destination, and then make a break for it. That way you might even learn something that could help Harry.

If you try to escape now, turn to page 12.

*If you wait for a better chance,
turn to page 100.*

84

"Harry," you say, "if you put the bins out on the back road, we won't be able to watch for vandals. If they're in front, at least we can see if someone's tampering with them."

"Forget it," says Harry. "I'm not putting them in front, and that's final."

You know what that tone of voice means. Getting the fruit out by train is not going to be possible unless you betray the secret of the crew, and you know you can't do that.

"There must be another alternative," you say.

Harry looks over at you. "I wish there were," he says sadly.

Suddenly you have an idea. "Harry!" you say. "If we can't get the crop to the consumers, let's get the consumers to the crop!"

"What do you mean?"

"Leave the bins in the orchard. When the pickers are done, you have a peach party right here on the farm. I'll make up posters and put them up in town, and we can hand out flyers at all the motels and campgrounds."

A grin slides over Harry's face. "Mrs. Winters can get some of her friends together and they can bake peach pies . . ."

"And we can make peach ice cream . . ."

"And set up tables on the lawn! It's a great idea! We'll have flats of peaches for sale for people to take home for canning."

"We may not move them all," you say to Harry, "but we'll sell a lot, and we won't have to rely on the truckers!"

Turn to page 16.

You decide to trust Belinda. "I've never been to sacred ground," you tell her.

She reaches for your hand. "Come," she says. "The ancestors will be kind to you, for they know you saved my life."

She leads you through the last orchard and across a field to the base of the hills. The ground is covered in deep underbrush, which makes the route difficult as you start to climb uphill. Soon you reach a pass that cuts through the rough terrain. It leads to a small mountain meadow that can't be seen from the orchards or the field. The storm clouds have blown to the east and the moon shines brightly, reflecting off the drops of water clinging to the blades of grass and turning the meadow into a silver fairyland.

Turn to page 103.

You turn around and run back toward the house. You don't know what the people in the barn are doing, but you're sure it's not good. Two sets of footsteps pound behind you. You're grabbed from behind and your arms are pinned back. The lantern falls from your hand.

"Snoop!" Chuck's voice hisses in your ear. "You'll learn to mind your own business!"

"What were you doing to Harry's tractor?" you demand, trying to wiggle out of Chuck's grasp.

"I'll ask the questions," says Chuck. He starts to drag you over toward his pickup truck, but suddenly a shot rings out. Chuck lets go of you and dives into the cab of the truck. His friend leaps in on the passenger side. You look around quickly to see who fired the shot.

Turn to page 15.

You slosh along through the orchard to the piece of track where you're supposed to meet the yellow dog and the train. You're early, but you want to be ready. You light the lantern and lean up against a tree to wait, peering through the darkness.

It seems as if you've been waiting forever when you hear a low growl come from the other side of the track. You hold up the lantern. From the north side of the property, you hear a faint whistle. You see a yellow blur moving through the shadows as the dog approaches. As you move toward the track, a voice calls out behind you.

"Stop! Halt! You're trespassing!"

It's the guard, Chuck. He can't tell that it's you. You know he's carrying a rifle, but would he dare shoot? He's going to ruin everything!

The train whistle blows again, and the dog barks. But you know Chuck can't hear or see either one. You don't have much time.

"Halt!" Chuck cries again.

Should you identify yourself to Chuck and risk losing the dog, or should you concentrate on the dog and hope that Chuck doesn't decide to shoot you?

If you stop and identify yourself, turn to page 4.

If you go after the dog, turn to page 28.

"No thanks," you say to Belinda. "I've had enough excitement for one night. I'm going back to the house. Good night."

You turn and start walking. But your head is full of questions. What was in Belinda's bundle? Why was she so adamant about having Harry hold on to that scrubby piece of land? What did she mean when she said that there was a 'shadow on your life'?

You grin. The farther you get from Belinda, the more absurd her predictions begin to sound, and the more you believe she was working in cahoots with the Naldo men. It must have all been an act to fool you.

You're so deep in thought as you pass the picker's cabin that you don't see or hear the men hiding in the bushes. They grab you from behind, clap a chloroform-soaked cloth over your nose, and load you into a waiting truck.

When the authorities in Austin, Texas pick you up for vagrancy, you have no identification and no recollection of who you are. Your life is like a shadow.

You are sent to a care facility and then to a series of foster homes, but you never find your real parents. The only stirring of memory you have comes when you see a TV documentary. Something about peach farming in British Columbia rings a bell. Though you try to remember why, you never do.

The End

"Canoe?" the Indian woman repeats. "Your canoe sank."

"No," you reply. "We hung on to the hull until you arrived." As you turn around to point toward the canoe, you let out a gasp. Silhouetted against the pale light of dawn is the awesome shape of a sea serpent!

You stare at it, aware now that you must have been clinging to one of its many protrusions, mistaking it for the hollowed-out log canoe.

"Ogopogo," you say quietly as everything turns dark. "There really is an Ogopogo."

When you open your eyes, you find yourself lying on the balcony. Harry is standing in the doorway grinning at you.

"Ogopogo, is it? Well, right now it's time for breakfast," Harry says, "but we can go to Lake Okanagan and check out Ogopogo this afternoon. Maybe we'll rent a canoe."

"No thanks!" you say. "I don't think I want to be out there on anything smaller than a freighter!"

The End

92

"I don't believe in spirits," you repeat, staring at the light, hypnotized. Suddenly, the light leaps toward you. You feel heat as it brushes your arm. "Get it away from me!" you yell hysterically, flailing at the ball of light with your hands.

"Calm down! Calm down!" Harry's voice booms out in the dark. He grabs your shoulders and shakes you. "Calm down! Who are you yelling at?"

"Belinda!" you scream. "Make her take those lights away!"

"Belinda went into town an hour ago," Harry says. "What lights are you talking about? It's black as pitch outside."

At that point you realize that you're in your room upstairs. But how did you get there? You don't sleep well that night, or the next one. And you're so nervous in the daytime that you're not much help to Harry. After a week, you reach a mutual decision that you should return home.

Months later, the golden dancing lights that have been haunting you finally disappear from your mind. However, the red, feather-shaped scar on your arm, where the dancing light burned you, never disappears. And although you don't know what happened, you know you'll never again deny the possibility of a spirit world.

The End

"And the rock?" you ask Belinda.

"The rock is to mark the place where we have been, so those who follow will know the way."

She moves back to the mouth of the pass and places the rock on the ground. "Mark carefully where I have laid it," she says.

You don't understand why you should do this, but you take a second look at where she has placed the rock.

"Come," she says. "We must return now. I am glad we had this time together. I will not be here much longer."

"What do you mean?" you ask. "Are you going somewhere?"

"Yes," she says. "To another place."

Suddenly a flash of lightning silhouettes the hills, and thunder rumbles ominously. Another storm is moving in. Fat raindrops begin to fall.

"The crop will not survive," Belinda says, looking skyward.

"It's just a thunderstorm," you say.

"No," she says, "it is more. The ancestors are speaking." She raises her hand in salute as she turns to go into the picker's cabin. "Remember the place of the rock," she says. "Good-bye."

You run the last hundred yards back to the house. You are drenched and shivering. It feels as if the temperature has dropped twenty degrees in the last half hour. You barely make it inside before hailstones the size of marbles come crashing to earth from the black sky. You take a hot shower and crawl into bed exhausted.

Turn to page 69.

94

Two days after your encounter with the phantom train, Harry comes home from the hospital. Since he has limited mobility on his crutches, you and Mrs. Winters turn his downstairs office into a bedroom.

Harry is in a bad mood most of the time. He spends hours on the phone talking to other growers about the possible truckers' strike. When you tell him the jeep tire blowout was caused by a rifle shot, he hires a guard—a man named Chuck Simpson—to patrol the farm. But even with Chuck on the job, you continue to find irrigation pipe that has been cut.

You wonder about your meeting with the train. Will the dog show up? Will you be able to get him aboard the coach? Did it all really happen, or were you just dreaming?

Turn to page 101.

When you go to bed that night, you lie awake for a long time. Sicamous! Right at the end of the run for the phantom train! You know the crew will help if you can contact them, but now that the curse has been lifted, signaling with the lantern may not work. The train may not be able to pass through time zones anymore. But the more you think about it, the more you realize you have to give it a try.

The next night, after Harry has gone to sleep, you take the lantern and go down to the orchard below the house. A little before ten, you start signaling, waving the lantern back and forth in an arc. A few minutes later you hear the whistle and see the wavering light of the engine. It worked!

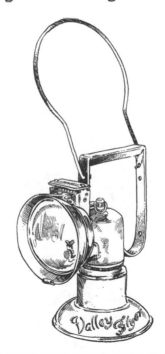

Turn to page 67.

You tuck the drawing into your shirt pocket. You're convinced that it means Chuck is working for Naldo. Business is slow and you're impatient to close so you can get back and tell Harry of your suspicions.

When Chuck finally arrives a little after five-thirty, you're waiting out in front with the cashbox in your hand.

"Well, you're in a rush to quit work!" he says. "Load the fruit." He takes the cashbox and thumbs through the bills. "Not much here," he says. "Maybe you're skimming some off the top."

"I wouldn't take Harry's money!" you say angrily.

"Of course not," Chuck says sarcastically. "What's that sticking out of your pocket?" He reaches over and snatches the drawing from your shirt pocket.

"Give that back!" you yell. But you're too late. Chuck has already unfolded the drawing and is studying it.

"What do you know about this?" he says.

"Nothing. It's something Belinda drew, I guess. I didn't pay much attention to it."

"I'm glad," Chuck says. He wads up the drawing, reaches into his pocket for a match, and sets it ablaze. "That's that! Now you won't have to pay any attention to it at all. Ever. Get it?"

Turn to page 83.

"There was a developer out there this morning," you lie. "He's willing to pay big bucks for that piece of land. He's talking about putting in a lodge, and ski lifts, and a big dining hall, and a swimming pool, and a . . ."

"Hotel?" says the attorney.

"Yes!" you reply.

"Satellite TV?" says Mr. Fox.

"Yes!"

"And a sushi bar?"

"Yes! . . . No, wait a minute." You look at their faces. "You're making fun of me," you say. Even Harry is laughing at you.

"Nice try," Harry says, signing the paper the lawyer puts in front of him. "I wish it were true. But none of that could happen without roads and water and sewers and electricity, and I don't think the township's ready to go to that expense. Mr. Fox is going to use it as a wilderness camp . . . a getaway."

Turn to page 116.

You feel the train slowing as it veers off onto a siding and stops. Strong hands help you to sit up. The engineer smiles at you. "That was very brave of you, to try to save the dog," he says.

"I don't get it," you say. "What happened? Where is the dog? And where did this train come from? Harry says the Valley Line hasn't run for over fifty years. Then all of a sudden I see you going through the orchard . . ." You shake your head in confusion. "I must be dreaming," you continue. "It's as if I've jumped back in time."

"You're not dreaming," Ben says. "And you haven't jumped back in time. You've just moved sideways."

"Sideways?" you ask.

Ben nods. "Most people don't understand that all time lines run parallel."

"What do you mean?" you ask, more confused than ever.

"Well, for example, the nineteenth, twentieth, and twenty-first centuries are all occurring at the same time. So are the decades of the twenties and the thirties and the nineties. They're all populated by different people. But once in a while something will happen that allows someone—in this case, you—to move between time lines."

"Do you know what happened?" you ask.

The men exchange glances.

Turn to page 18.

100

You decide to wait for a better opportunity to escape, and find out as much as you can in the meantime.

"Who's the real boss?" you ask Chuck.

"You'll find out soon enough," he says. You drive for several miles through a densely forested area and turn off on a side road. Soon you are passing rows of cherry trees. A large house sits at the end of the road. Beyond the house are several outbuildings. Chuck drives past the house toward a long, low building. A truck with a Naldo emblem meets you halfway down the lane. The driver waves at Chuck. It's the same man you saw on the highway this morning.

"I'm taking the kid to the bunkhouse until dark," Chuck yells.

The driver nods and signals for him to pass.

Turn to page 79.

The day you're supposed to meet the train is rainy—not a gentle summer rain, but a torrential downpour that threatens the peach crop and makes Harry even more surly. You're glad when dinner's over.

"Think I'll go upstairs and read," you tell Harry.

He nods but doesn't look up from the papers he's working on. "Good night," he mutters. "I'll be turning in soon myself."

You lie down on your bed with a book. But you don't read. You watch the clock. At nine-forty you pick up the lantern, loop a piece of rope around your belt, and creep downstairs. In your back pocket is a piece of rawhide to use as a lure for the dog.

No light is showing under the door to Harry's room. You go outside. It has stopped raining and the air is fresh, but overhead the sky is dark. The night feels ominous.

Turn to page 88.

"It's beautiful," you say.

"Yes," Belinda agrees. She drops to her knees and bends low, touching her forehead to the ground. She then begins to chant in a low voice, and you know that she is calling on her ancestors. When she is through, she reaches for the bundle. You lean forward for a better look, but as she unfolds the corners of the cloth, you're disappointed. The precious bundle she's been carrying contains some very ordinary things: a feather, a piece of rock, a peach pit, and a clump of dirt.

As if sensing your disappointment, Belinda turns to you. "Each has its place," she says. "The feather gives us wings between this life and the next . . . the pit perpetuates the growth of all things. . . ." She breaks up the clump of earth and lets it sift through her fingers. "Warm earth to plant it in . . ."

She lays each item on the ground as she speaks.

Turn to page 93.

Harry waits until the motor in Chuck's pickup truck starts up and then pushes open the barn door with one of his crutches. He hands you the rifle. "I can go a lot faster if you carry this. Let's see what was going on in here."

"When did you begin to suspect Chuck?"

Harry grins at you. "I started keeping an eye on him right after you tipped me to your suspicions," he says. He flicks on a light switch and goes over to the tractor.

"What are you looking for?" you ask.

"I want to check the hydraulic line on the forklift," he says. "Could be very dangerous if they monkey with that." He looks behind the tractor and points with his crutch. "What's that?"

"That's the bag the other guy had," you say, handing it to Harry. "He must have dropped it. He may still be around."

"I don't think so," Harry says, pouring something white out of the bag and into his hand. "They're cowards. They don't want open confrontation."

"That looks like sugar!"

"It is," says Harry. "Doesn't take much of this to mess up an engine. Lucky I have a locking cap on the gas tank. Let's go turn in. We have a busy day ahead of us tomorrow."

When you get back to the house, you fix some hot chocolate and take it in to Harry. You notice that he has propped the rifle within easy reach of his bed. He's also put an extension cord on the downstairs phone. Better safe than sorry.

Turn to page 110.

"Go inside and call the constable," Harry says to you, "while I check the equipment. That's what they were after."

When you come back out of the house, Belinda is gone and Harry is now guarding the two men. A few minutes later the police come and take them away. You and Harry then go inside.

"Harry," you say, "I don't understand how Belinda managed to reappear like that, just in time to catch the saboteurs."

"Neither do I," says Harry. "Some things can't be explained."

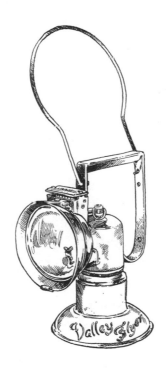

Turn to page 48.

"I'll help you if I can," you tell the crew of the train. "But there's something I don't understand. Belinda, the shaman, is living in my time zone. If her dog gets back to the correct time zone, will she go back automatically?"

"We don't know," Jeremiah says. "She passes through time frequently. We've seen her as we go up and down the valley. But she can't reclaim her dog until it's in the right time zone. It can't get back without your help, and neither can we."

"What do I have to do?" you ask.

"One week from tonight," Ben replies, "is the anniversary of the dog's accident with the train. We think he'll be back on the track, waiting. We want you to be there, too. Deliver the dog to us, and we'll take it from there."

"I'll do my best," you say. "What time?"

"When the clock strikes ten, you'll hear the whistle," says Ben. "Have the dog in your grasp by the third blast. We'll slow down to get him aboard. Saul will be watching for you. But you mustn't tell anyone about us. Not a soul!"

"I won't. I promise," you say.

They back the train off the siding and let you off just below the house. Clutching the lantern in one hand, you swing down from the engine. The moment your feet touch the wet grass in the field, the train vanishes. Once again the track is overgrown with grass and weeds. There's no sign at all that a train has passed through.

You shiver. It's late and you're tired, but you don't sleep very well.

Turn to page 94.

"Are you Mariana?" you ask, standing up to follow her.

"Yes," she replies softly. "Come with me. Hurry!"

You pull on a pair of jeans over your pajamas. Mariana leads you down the two flights of stairs to the ground floor and out through the back entrance. As you follow her along the side of the house, you notice that Harry's station wagon is gone. In its place is an old farm wagon.

"Wait a minute!" you say. "Where are we going?"

"To find my beloved," she says.

Suddenly, you are both seized from behind. You twist around to look and see that your captors are two Indian braves. Two more Indians lead horses from the bushes. Mariana speaks to the men sharply, but you don't understand her words or their replies.

They tie her hands and then yours and force you to mount the horses. With a brave seated behind each of you, you gallop off in the direction of Lake Okanagan.

More Indians await you at the shore of the lake. Swiftly and without discussion, you and Mariana are taken from the horses, put in a canoe hollowed from a tree trunk, and set adrift on the lake.

Clouds cover the moon and stars, and a stiff wind off the Rockies stirs up waves that move the canoe farther and farther out onto the lake. Back on shore, your Indian captors are chanting and singing around a bonfire.

Turn to page 76.

108

The hot metal of the balcony railing burns into your hands, and you bite your lip to keep from crying out. You hang there—the fire in front of you and the mob below—until the railing starts to bend from the heat and the weight of your body.

You let go.

When you wake up, you're in a hospital room. Your right leg is in a cast, and your hands are bandaged. Harry is standing by the window talking in whispers to a woman in a white coat.

"I can't really say how it happened, doctor," you overhear Harry say. "I did tell the story about Mariana, but . . ."

"The power of suggestion can be magnified in the dream state," the doctor says. "My guess would be that the youngster was reenacting the story and fell from the balcony while sleepwalking."

"But there's something I don't understand," Harry says.

"What's that?" asks the doctor.

"The burns. The burns on the hands."

The doctor shrugs. "I'm afraid I don't know," she says, shaking her head. "I can come up with no medical answer for that. There's no logical reason I can think of, either."

You open your mouth to explain what happened, but you realize you don't have any answers yourself. "I think the time has come," you hear Harry say softly, "to board up the attic room."

The End

110

You sleep restlessly. You don't know how you're going to get the fruit loaded onto the train without telling Harry, but you promised the crew you wouldn't reveal their secret to anyone. When you go downstairs in the morning, Harry is already up and arguing with Mrs. Winters about something.

"Dr. Morrow isn't going to be pleased to hear that you're out traipsing through the orchards, Harry Westlake!" Mrs. Winters says. "He told you no fieldwork for six weeks!"

"Dr. Morrow isn't going to hear about it unless you go and tell him," Harry replies.

Mrs. Winters flips the bacon out of the pan. "Well, of course, I'm not going to tell him," she says huffily. "But I do worry!"

Harry hobbles over to her and puts his arm around her shoulder. "I know," he says. "It's for my own good, right?"

"Right," says Mrs. Winters.

None of you talk very much at breakfast.

"Ready?" Harry asks, when you take your dishes to the sink.

"Ready," you reply.

The pickers are already arriving. The day is a whirlwind of activity, as bin after bin of peaches is filled.

"It's a good crop," Harry says. "Tomorrow we'll move the bins to the loading dock on the back road."

"Back road?" you say. "What about the front dock, the one on the road leading to the high-way?"

Turn to page 35.

The next morning Harry hollers to you before your alarm goes off. At first you think you're dreaming, but when Mrs. Winters taps on the bedroom door, you know it's no dream. You hop out of bed and open the door.

"Hurry down, dear," she says. "Harry needs you."

You throw on your clothes and run downstairs, wondering what the fuss is about. Harry is in the office eating breakfast. He pushes a plate of bacon and eggs toward you.

"Here, eat up!" he says. "Sorry about the rush, but we're short staffed today. I need you to go work in the fruit stand."

"But Belinda . . ." you start to say.

"Belinda has disappeared," Harry says. "When she didn't come to pick up the cashbox at six-thirty, I sent Mrs. Winters over with it. Belinda's gone, lock, stock and barrel. The picker's cabin is so clean it looks like she never lived there."

Of course! Belinda's gone back to the other time zone with the dog! A big grin crosses your face as you put the pieces together. That means it really did happen. And the trainmen are now back with their families.

"What are you grinning at?" Harry asks.

"Oh, I'm just looking forward to working in the fruit stand," you tell him. "It will be . . . different."

"Here's the cashbox," Harry says. "Chuck's waiting outside to give you a ride to the stand."

Turn to page 27.

112

You stare at your hand; it's beginning to swell. "Help me!" you yell, panicking. "I must be allergic to whatever bit me!" You turn to Belinda accusingly. "You did this!" you say. "You put a curse on me, didn't you? I could die. You're evil!" Your whole arm is swelling now, and your skin is beginning to turn blue. You're having difficulty breathing.

Belinda ignores your accusations and turns to the tourist. "Can you help?" she asks the man calmly.

"I'll get my bag," he says, rushing to his car.

You watch with relief. What a lucky break—the man buying fruit is a doctor!

The doctor gives you two injections and your breathing almost immediately becomes easier and the swelling starts to recede. After he drives away, you turn to Belinda.

"It's a good thing that the doctor was here when you made that bug bite me," you say angrily. "What a lucky coincidence."

Belinda stares back at you. "You will learn," she says, "that there is no such thing as coincidence. Coincidence is the way the spirits stay anonymous."

"Are you saying that you arranged to have that doctor here?" you ask.

"The more one talks about what one can do," Belinda repeats, "the less one is able to do."

Turn to page 14.

114

You decide to call Dr. Morrow. Later that evening, while Harry is busy in another room, you place the call from the kitchen phone. When his exchange answers, you tell them that it's an emergency. In a few minutes, you have Dr. Morrow on the line.

"Dr. Morrow," you say, disguising your voice. "This is a friend of Harry Westlake. I'm worried about him. He's out in the orchard every day. He doesn't keep his leg elevated and . . ."

"What is this?" asks a voice behind you. You turn around slowly. Harry is standing there, listening. He takes the receiver, says a few words to Dr. Morrow, and hangs up.

"I think you've got some explaining to do," Harry says to you. "You'd better have an awfully good reason for wanting me to be housebound for the next few days."

You look down at the floor. "I'm sorry," you say, "I do have a good reason, but I can't tell you what it is."

"That sounds intriguing," Harry says. "As I see it, you have two options. One, you can tell me why you made that call. Or two, you can go upstairs and pack your bag."

Go on to the next page.

You turn away and look out the window. You feel trapped. In order to help Harry, you'll have to betray the men on the train. If you choose to go home, you'll have accomplished nothing at all. Harry will certainly lose the crop, and probably the farm, too.

"Well?" says Harry.

You have no choice. "I'll tell you, but I'm warning you, you're not going to believe me. It's a weird story. Let's sit down."

Turn to page 56.

But apparently Mr. Fox liked your idea better. After he buys the land, he talks the township into putting in electricity and water and sewers. The province puts in a road, and Mr. Fox sells the piece of land for ten times what he paid Harry for it. Within five years, Harry's scruffy orchard is a thriving winter resort, with ski runs, a lodge, and a swimming pool. The new owner becomes a millionaire.

Harry sells the rest of the farm to the new owner for a fabulous amount and moves to the coast.

Years later, you become an adviser to major corporations, specializing in real estate. With a little luck and a lot of creativity, you have an amazing success rate in predicting future trends.

The End

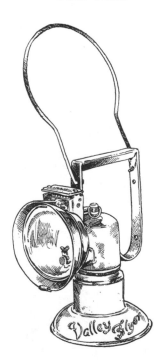

ABOUT THE AUTHOR

LOUISE MUNRO FOLEY is the author of many books in the Choose Your Own Adventure series, including *The Cobra Connection*. Her books have been published in several languages, including Danish, Spanish, and Japanese. She has written for radio, television, and newspapers in the United States and Canada. A native of Toronto, Canada, Ms. Foley now lives in Sacramento, California. She has two sons.

ABOUT THE ILLUSTRATOR

FRANK BOLLE studied at Pratt Institute. He has worked as an illustrator for many national magazines and now creates and draws cartoons for magazines as well. He has also worked in advertising and children's educational materials and has drawn and collaborated on several newsaper comic strips, including *Annie* and *Winnie Winkle*. He has illustrated many books in the Choose Your Own Adventure series, including *Master of Kung Fu, South Pole Sabotage, Return of the Ninja, You Are a Genius, Through the Black Hole, The Worst Day of Your Life, Master of Tae Kwon Do, The Cobra Connection, Hijacked!, Master of Karate, Invaders from Within, The Lost Ninja, Daredevil Park, Kidnapped!,* and *The Terrorist Trap*. A native of Brooklyn Heights, New York, Mr. Bolle now lives and works in Westport, Connecticut.